For my beloved

Stay crazy, dream big and always inspire

Intergalactic Games: Victory for Doomshot

For information contact:

(London/Manchester: dsarsalem@gmail.com)

Book and Cover design by HK Salem

First Edition: January 2022

AUTHOR

HK was born and raised in England and trained as a Molecular Biologist. During his career he was involved in cutting-edge research. HK uses his deep understanding and knowledge of the cellular basis of life, the secret histories of the universe, mystical teachings of ancient and current schools of wisdom and his platform as an international motivational speaker to create stories with deep and profound meaning that capture the imaginations of readers of all ages, drawing them into alternative worlds where *good vs. bad* battles take stage in epic style!

Content

Book Blurb

"Brandon narrowly avoids the fire-spitting dragon, dodges the one-eyed charging bull, shimmies the ball past a *Rhinosapien*, and majestically lifts the ball with his gifted right foot and volleys the ball towards the top corner of the net after invoking a hurricane thundershot spell – the ecstatic crowds are on their feet!"

Brandon, a young boy from London, is frustrated with his parents, who spend all their time working – which means no time for anything else, especially him. Mostly he *really* misses playing football with Dad. It used to be the best time in the world for him. But recently, with his dad needing to be away more and more, Brandon finds his own world falling apart, until he discovers a hidden secret about the family…

Join Brandon as he unravels the family secrets which will lead him into a fantasy adventure, which leads him to understanding his love for football. He will learn about the secret history of football and will join the famous Doomshot Academy: Wizardry School for Footballers.

CHAPTER 1

Brandon is not a happy boy!

Brandon was upset. No, he was angry! Steam was coming out of his ears, and his face was turning BEETROOT RED! Dad was leaving on yet another work trip and would be away for at least two weeks. He was going to miss the big England game! He had promised they would go together and watch this one live. He had been waiting months for this game and it was all he had thought about and talked about for those last few months. For Dad to now say they wouldn't be able to go because of work – AGAIN! – was crushing.

Dad tried his best to explain the situation to Brandon, but Brandon turned away angrily. He was tired of hearing his excuses! He leapt up to grab his favourite scruffy, muddy Adidas trainers, ran downstairs and dashed out into the back garden. He was getting all too used to the disappointment of Dad's failed promises. His ball, glimmering from the shiny silver stripes reflecting the sun rays, caught his attention from the corner of his eye, and he walked over to it, dragging his feet sullenly. He began rolling the ball under and then over his right foot and started his keepie-uppies. This usually helped him calm down, his go-to-thing when he was upset, but this time it wasn't helping.

As he flicked the ball up and down, kicking it above his shoulder height, Brandon watched it as it majestically came down. As he did this repeatedly, suddenly the background noises of the outdoors seemed to go strangely quiet. The rage that had been building inside him was clear to see by the expression on his face. As the ball slowly fell to his waist level, he struck it on the volley with his favourite right foot and really belted it with all the strength he could muster. He focused all his anger now and connected perfectly. The ball smashed towards the goal that Dad had set up for him at the end of the garden. Brandon remarked to himself, *That must be the hardest I've ever kicked it!*

As the ball whizzed through the air, time appeared to slow down. The skies darkened, with an almost instant gathering of grey clouds above him, and electricity sparked out from the edges of the ball as it whizzed towards the net of the goal. Just as the ball headed into the top corner of the net, a blast of light and smoke appeared, producing a mysterious black hole that swallowed the ball! An eerie voice echoed from beyond the darkened clouds. "Brandon…it's time for you to fulfil your destiny..."

And just like that, the dark clouds cleared, the sky returned to bright blue sunshine, but Brandon's ball had disappeared! Brandon stood still in complete disbelief. *What just happened?* he thought to himself. Brandon looked around to see if anyone else saw what he saw, but no one was there. He ran in to tell Mum, but she replied, "Don't worry, you'll get your ball back if it went over the neighbours' fence."

"It didn't go over, Mum," Brandon protested. "It

disappeared into some kind of a magical black hole!"

Mum, who as always wasn't listening, just smiled, and said, "Come in now and wash your hands. It's time for dinner."

Brandon went over to the sink and began washing his hands, still baffled and confused by what had just happened.

CHAPTER 2

Dreams of a footballer

Brandon sat quietly throughout dinner. Mum and Dad were busy chatting about their plans for the next few days. Dad was going through his complex travel itinerary, waving his hands around in overly animated gestures, whilst Mum was making mental notes (aloud!) about an important presentation she was due to give in front of many important people. Safiya, Brandon's little sister, was chatting away as always, asking many crazy questions that Mum and Dad always loved to answer. Safiya was what Brandon liked to call a 'total chatter box'. She was only a year and a half younger than Brandon, and was clearly Dad's little princess, who loved reading...a lot! Safiya would read literally just about anything she could find that had words on it, and then had to ask any adult (or Brandon when no adults were around), what EVERY word meant, which was usually followed by "but why?"

Brandon sat at the table staring out the window, oblivious to the things going on around him. He ate his food, politely asked if he could be excused from the table and made his way upstairs to his bedroom. As he looked around, still lost in his own thoughts, Brandon collapsed backwards on his bed with an explosive sigh.

His bedroom was full of all his favourite things - football and fantasy memorabilia. On one wall he had posters of Arsenal players and the Emirates stadium and in between, he had pictures of Avengers and all kinds of fantasy characters. Ever since Brandon could remember he had been obsessed with football. He loved everything about the game and could literally spend all day and night just kicking the ball and playing. He always thought there was something magical about the way some of his heroes like Messi and Mo Salah could run and play. On rainy days, Brandon would often play with his fantasy figures, lining them up on his football carpet and imagining his own fantasy football game.

As Brandon lay on his bed, looking up at the ceiling, he thought about the new school year which was about to start tomorrow. He fervently hoped this year he was going to make it into the school football team, especially after the disappointment of last year, when he missed being selected for the squad. Brandon was a little bit smaller than most of the other boys and he was told that he was not big or strong enough and that he would get hurt. This was so unfair and if only Mr Bumkins, the school coach, would give him a chance, he knew he could show them what he could do.

Brandon was determined to show them this time

what he could do. As Brandon thought about the trials coming up that first week, he began to forget about the disappointment of missing the England game with Dad and started to drift off to sleep…

CHAPTER 3

Football trials at school and a fight

Brandon woke up the next morning to find the house in chaos. Mum was frantically trying to jump between making breakfast, which was on fire, and making lunch for Brandon and Safiya. Safiya was playing with her unicorn teddy and was completely oblivious to the time, and all he could hear was Mum shouting at her to get her teeth brushed. Brandon got up to see if Dad was there because he wanted to ask him about trying a new skill, but when he went into his room, he found Dad had already left.

Brandon brushed his teeth, got ready super quick and came down to have breakfast. Mum had packed his bag already, but Brandon had to double-check she had packed his favourite boots. She had put the wrong ones in! Brandon shouted to her, "Mum, you put the wrong boots in!" Brandon took out the ones in the bag and reached above the shelf to grab his favourite ones. Dad had stuck a Post-it note on the right boot which read "Good luck with the trials today, Brandon. Remember you are gifted and you can do anything you put your mind (and right boot) to!" Brandon smiled, but almost instantly became sad again. Dad used to watch all his games when he was little, but lately, he was never around and Brandon missed seeing Dad's face at the games on the sidelines. Mum shouted at Brandon to hurry up and get in the car.

As Brandon pulled up to school and walked through the gates, he waved goodbye to Mum and Safiya and walked in. All through class, Brandon was daydreaming. Suddenly Brandon was brought back to reality by the sound of the bell and Mr Bumkins telling him he was going to miss the trials if he didn't get a move on.

Brandon grabbed his bag and ran through the corridors to reach the changing rooms. A group of boys were already in their gear and chatting and laughing out loud. Brandon took his kit out and started to suit up. When he took his boots out, one of the boys started making fun of his old boots. "Are you so poor, Brandon, that you can't afford new boots? Those are so rubbish and dirty!!" He encouraged the other boys to laugh too.

Brandon stared sternly and replied, "Oh shut up! Let's just see what happens on the pitch, shall we?"

The other boy tried punch Brandon and started a fight. Brandon lobbed a blow at him and missed, and then a scrap started. The other boys formed a ring and started chanting, "Fight, fight, fight."

Mr Bumkins came in and separated them. He warned them all that fighting was not acceptable and there would be consequences! He then ordered everyone out to the fields and the trials began.

Brandon played extremely well. He performed all the drills perfectly and scored points on all the exercises. He did some of his favourite tricks that Dad had taught him during the summer and everyone watching was cheering. Mr Bumkins then ended the trials by blowing his whistle and told everyone to get changed and the squad would be announced tomorrow on the notice board.

As Brandon was leaving, he saw the dad of the other boy he had just fought with arrive in his brand new Mercedes. The man got out and approached Mr Bumkins. They shook hands, laughed and talked. Brandon couldn't hear what was said. Then they both looked across at Brandon, and the man pointed at him and then carried on chatting with Mr Bumkins.

Brandon saw Mum waiting and waving. He ran over to her. Seeing Mum's big smile and, of course, the snacks and special treat she held, always cheered Brandon up, and he forgot all about the scrap and even the trial! Brandon stared out of the window all the way home, daydreaming about something with a smile on his face.

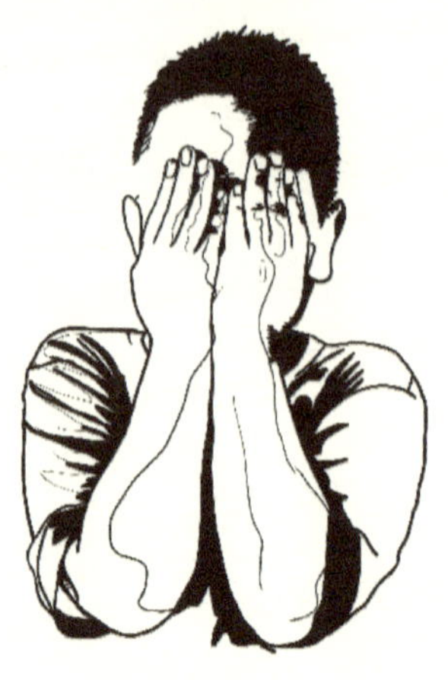

CHAPTER 4

Life is so unfair

The next morning, Brandon jumped out of bed. Today he would find out about the squad. He knew he had done his best yesterday and that it had been enough to get selected. The normal routine of chaos and screaming from Mum continued, but Brandon was too preoccupied to notice any of the noise. He was already sitting in the car before Mum could tell him. He just wanted to get to school to check the notice boards.

As Mum pulled up outside the school gates, Brandon ran off without even waving goodbye. He ran straight into the school corridors and towards the notice board. He scanned all the different notices and looked for the football squad announcement. He saw the list! He ran over and started to run his finger down it. 1…2…he scanned all the way down to number 18. His name wasn't there! *What?* He looked shocked. Then he saw his name at the bottom, with a note that said to come and meet Mr Bumkins immediately before registration.

He went to Mr Bumkins' office and knocked on the door. Mr Bumkins sat Brandon down and explained that because he started a fight with the other boy, he was not being selected for the squad. Brandon protested that it wasn't his fault, but Mr Bumkins said it was too late and he should try again next year.

"Next year!?" Brandon screamed in protest. "I can't wait another year—what about the other boy?" He had seen his name on the list; why was he included? Mr

Bumkins explained that his father was a very important man and supported the school and it was all arranged with the headmaster. Brandon said this was so unfair, but that was that and nothing could change Mr Bumkins' mind.

Brandon was devastated. All day he walked from class to class, miserable. Life was so unfair!

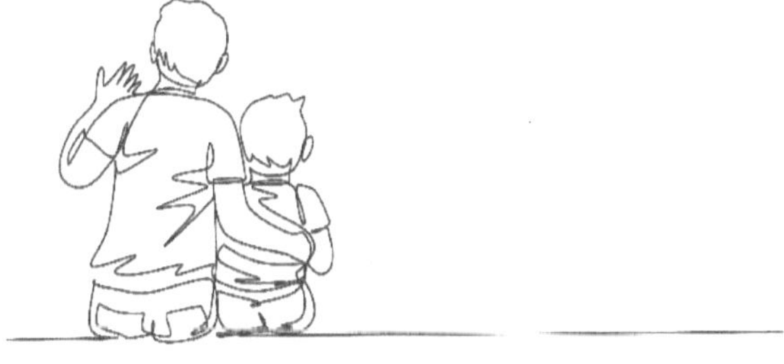

CHAPTER 5

Granddad to the rescue

Brandon came home that evening, and Mum knew straight away that something wasn't right. She tried to ask Brandon what was wrong but he didn't want to talk.

Then Mum said, "Why don't you go up and get changed for tea time? Oh, by the way, there's a surprise for you waiting upstairs in your room."

Brandon looked up questioningly. "What is it?"

"Well, go up and look," Mum said.

Brandon ran up the stairs and found Granddad waiting in his room. A giant smile spread across his face. He was always happy to see Granddad, and especially today, because of what happened at school. He ran up and gave him the biggest hug. Granddad asked him if everything was ok. Brandon burst into tears and told Granddad everything that happened, about the fight and about not being picked for the squad. Then Brandon went on to tell Granddad that Dad was never around and on top of everything he would now miss the England game too. Brandon shouted, "This is the worst week of my life!"

Granddad sat down with Brandon and told him that everything would be ok. "Don't worry about the school. I will speak to them and see what I can do." He then gave him the best news ever. He was going to take Brandon to watch the game instead of Dad. He pulled out two golden tickets from his back pocket and said, "These are very special tickets indeed..."

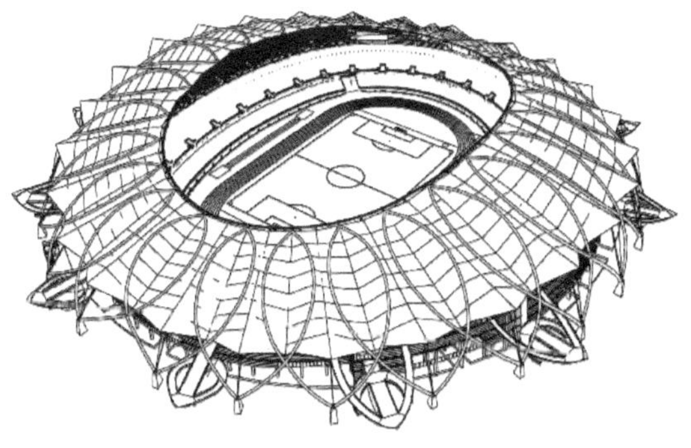

CHAPTER 6

On our way to Wembley!

The day of the big England game was here. Dad had called on Mum's phone using video calling and had spoken to Brandon. He said he would be home soon but for now Granddad would take him to the match and that he would have a very special day indeed. Dad always said things like that, so Brandon didn't really think much of it at the time.

Granddad walked ever so slowly up to Wembley stadium. He had a walking stick and Brandon sometimes got a little impatient, saying, "Hurry up or we'll be late, Granddad!"

Granddad just smiled and said, "Don't worry, we are exactly on time!"

Brandon looked at the signs and asked Granddad which entrance they should head for. Granddad pulled out the tickets and read out the ticket numbers. "Gate 11.1, turnstile 33.3." Brandon looked around but he couldn't find it anywhere. Granddad smiled and said, "Follow me. I'll show you where it is!"

He walked to the north gate and stood directly facing the Bobby Moore statue that stood proudly outside the stadium entrance. Brandon looked puzzled and agitated, as they were running late. Brandon turned his attention to Granddad and said, "Granddad, this is a great statue but we *really* need to get to our gate. What are we doing here?"

Granddad smiled and then started making circling gestures with his hands. Just as Brandon was about to ask Granddad again what on earth he was doing, the skies began to darken and everything around them began to slow down and go quiet. Sparks shot out around the circles that Granddad was making and suddenly a football appeared and hovered just above Brandon's foot. Granddad told Brandon to pass the ball as accurately as he could towards Bobby Moore. Brandon just stared at Granddad, very puzzled. *What is happening? Are you getting a bit old and crazy, Granddad?* thought Brandon.

Just then Brandon remembered the other day when he had kicked the ball in the garden and something similar had happened and the ball disappeared – he thought he had just imagined it that day, but was it happening again?

Granddad calmly told Brandon to do what he asked and everything would make sense.

Brandon lined himself up and with a mighty kick, he booted the ball forward. Suddenly, the statue of Bobby Moore came alive. It jumped down from the pedestal and controlled the zooming ball Brandon had kicked. Bobby signalled towards Brandon and Granddad to come to him. A short stairwell opened in the pedestal that Bobby Moore had jumped down from, revealing a previously hidden turnstile at the bottom with the number 33.3 showing above it. A strange-looking man, with a long pointy nose and tiny round spectacles said, "Tickets please?" He then said, "Hurry, the game is about to start!"

Granddad gave Brandon his ticket and told him to hand it to the strange man. Granddad said he would see him later but for now, Brandon had to go in alone and someone would meet him inside. Brandon looked scared, but Granddad reassured him he would be fine. Brandon went through. The door closed behind him and he could no longer see Granddad.

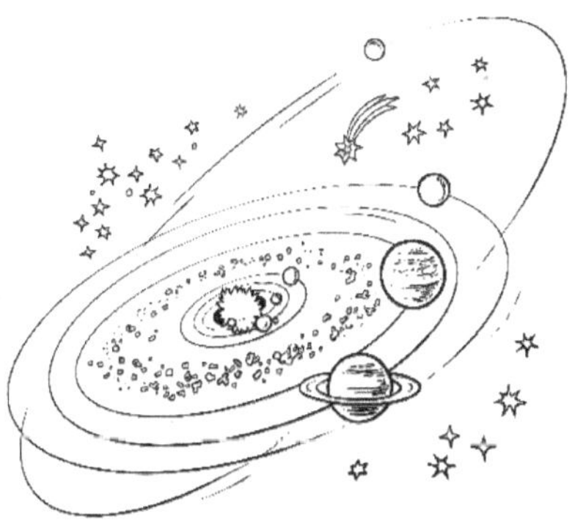

CHAPTER 7

Welcome to the Seventh Realm

Brandon was now standing in a place that didn't look like the inside of Wembley. In fact, it was completely different to any place that Brandon had ever seen! As he looked around him, he started to notice that things were not normal at all. The first thing Brandon noticed was the sky was a light shade of green, not blue, which looked like a reflection of the pitch at Wembley. Then he saw what looked like three suns—one purple, one blue and one red—set in an arch formation against the green sky. The air was cleaner, and Brandon breathed deeply and thought to himself it reminded him of the clean morning air when he went camping in the mountains. As Brandon began to realise he was not in a place that he recognised, he began to become more aware of his new surroundings.

Brandon stood at the edge of small road. In front of him, he saw crowds of people, and the area appeared to be getting busier by the minute, with more and more people coming and going, all dressed in different sports kits and wearing different team jerseys. It reminded him of the airport terminal where he often went to tell Dad goodbye as he headed off on his many trips.

Everyone was busy talking to each other or shouting instructions. It appeared that they were dropping off their family members, waving goodbye amid lots of tears from mothers and laughing between apparent friends. Then Brandon noticed a floating football! It just whizzed past him and placed itself inside the game bag of one of the people standing around.

Brandon noticed young boys and girls who had very special features. To his left he saw a family of three-legged people. They had purple scaly skin (like that on a lizard) but they smiled and talked just like Brandon did! To his right he saw a mum and dad dropping off their child – except they all had wings and floated very elegantly as they touched down near the side. They smiled at Brandon, and as Brandon waved towards them, rather shyly, they fluttered their wings as if to wave back to him.

As the sky glistened with the light of the three suns, he could see a faint magical glimmering dust whishing and whooshing just above the people, which Brandon thought reminded him of magic fairy dust from the books he used to read.

In the distance, Brandon noticed a man wearing what looked like a referee's uniform holding up a board that had his name written on it. Brandon raised his hands and shouted, "That's me! I'm Brandon!"

The man acknowledged Brandon with the sharp,

loud sound of a whistle that was hanging around his neck and came running up to Brandon. As he approached, Brandon noticed the whistle was in fact a small miniature football figurine which seemed to be alive itself. The mini figurine once again started making a whistling sound until the referee around whose neck he hung told him, "Stop that!" and the figurine looked upset and froze, morphing into a simple plastic whistle on a necklace.

The referee greeted Brandon and said, "Lovely to meet you, young Brandon. Now we must hurry. There are only eight minutes to spare and we must reach the gates before the whistle blows for registration."

Brandon was not sure what was happening, but the referee assured Brandon that his granddad had made all the arrangements, showing him a photo that he had of Granddad, so Brandon nodded and ran alongside until they arrived at the gates of a giant stadium. Above the gates was the name 'Doomshot Academy: Wizardry School for Footballers'. Behind the gates an enormous structure, as large as Wembley itself, stood majestically. It was a round bowl-like structure and had overarching towers on either side. There was a laser-projected covering which formed a force field-like mesh across the top. Fire intermittently blew out from the two sides and withdrew after two or three blows, only to restart again a few minutes later.

Brandon saw an enormous floating digital clock, like the kind one would see at a football game that counted down the time left in a game. The clock showed time countdown to the start of the Wizardry School Season.

Where am I? What is this place? Brandon thought to himself in amazement.

CHAPTER 8

Surprising stories about Dad

Brandon was rushed through the gates, where he was greeted by an extremely tall, athletic-looking man, with greasy, slicked-back black hair that formed a neat ponytail. His name was Coach Grundle. Coach Grundle extended his long skinny arm and shook Brandon's hand vigorously, saying, "C'mon young man, we haven't got long, and we need to get registered before the whistle blows."

Brandon stopped and said very politely but sternly,

"Sorry sir, but who are you??"

Coach Grundle said, "Oh, I'm sorry, I forgot to introduce myself, didn't I? I am an ex-team player and dear old friend of your dad. We played in the old days, in the battle games during the Darkside tournament and of course the Rebellion Games – phew, I tell you, they were some incredible times – but I guess your dad must have told you all about those, right?"

Brandon looked Coach Grundle straight in the eyes. "Excuse me, sir, but I think you must have me mixed up with someone else."

Coach Grundle looked at Brandon with a raised eyebrow. He asked Brandon if his dad had told him about 'Seventh Realm" and about why he was now here. Brandon shook his head from side to side, indicating he had no idea what it was or where he was now.

Coach Grundle said, "Oh dear…well Brandon, I guess it will come as quite a shock to know the fate of the universe rests on your shoulders now, huh?"

Brandon started breathing heavily and fell to the ground. Coach Grundle realised Brandon was having some sort of panic attack. He reached for a small brown paper bag that was in his pocket, handed it to Brandon and told him to breath into it nice and slow. Brandon calmed down.

Coach Grundle sat him down and said, "Let's get ourselves sorted out first and then we can sit over there," pointing to a huge tree surrounded by football-shaped seats, "and I will try and explain everything to you. I guess you must have a thousand and one questions! Oh dear…where to start?" grumbled Coach Grundle.

CHAPTER 9

History of the universe and the Gods of football

Coach Grundle and Brandon sat underneath the huge tree, which was known as the 'Fair-play Tree'. This tree was the wisest and most knowledgeable tree in all the universe. People would come from all over the galaxy to seek the profound wisdom the Fair-play Tree had to offer. The Fair-play Tree was an enormous tree that extended higher than the eye could see when standing below it. The trunk itself was so wide and twisted that it would take Brandon and at least 15 of his friends holding hands to reach all the way around. It was believed the roots extended far down into the depths of the planet's core. The roots touched all parts of the planet and the branches reached and twisted up like antennae that acted as satellites, connecting and communicating to all corners of the universe. It was believed the twisted nature of the tree trunk represented the changing nature of the times and people, and each branch and each twist told a tale of a time long ago. Undoubtedly this truly was the wisest tree in all the universe.

As Coach Grundle settled Brandon down, he began to explain…

"You come from a place called London, in a country called England on a continent called Europe on a planet called Earth. But Earth is a just one of many other planets."

Brandon jumped up and said, "Yes, I know about Mars and Jupiter and …"

"Yes, yes…but there are many other galaxies that exist in multiple dimensions," said Coach Grundle.

"These realms and galaxies and the planets that exist within them are like alternative versions of Earth and its own galaxy – the Milky Way. These dimensions were created before time existed and the balance of life in all these dimensions is sustained by the 'One Source Energy'."

Coach Grundle continued to explain, "In the beginning, before time, there were supreme beings that roamed the universe. These supreme beings invented games to keep themselves entertained. Of all the games they invented, football was their favourite. Why do you think all the planets are round, like footballs? Eventually, as time was created and the universe evolved, each supreme being created life on his own 'football-shaped planet' and soon the planets emerged with new life. These life forms began as plants and animals and eventually people, like me and you, but in some cases very different from me and you! These people began to populate the planet and soon the life forms learned the ways of their creator or supreme being and of course this meant they learned the game of football, and everyone learned to love the game of football!

"Whilst people enjoyed the game of the gods, they also became aware that their existence depended upon the One Source Energy that sustained their planet. When the people of each planet heard there was only one source of energy for everyone, they started panicking and wanted to control it for themselves. This led to wars starting between the planets. One day after the deadliest battle, it was decided that no more wars would occur, and the leaders of the planets would need to learn to share the One Source Energy by taking turns. In order to decide who would control the source, an intergalactic football tournament was created. The best footballers would be selected from each planet and would play in an intergalactic tournament. This worked very well for centuries, but over time, some groups on certain planets became evil and if they were to win the tournament they would abuse the power of controlling the One Source Energy and many planets would suffer and people would even die!"

Coach Grundle explained to Brandon that Earth was one of these planets that would certainly not survive if the evil group took control.

"So Brandon," said Coach Grundle, "just like your dad, granddad, great-granddad and your ancestors before him, who have all played in these great tournaments, you too may one day play for the survival of the planet Earth and to maintain the peaceful balance in the universe!" Coach Grundle jumped with excitement. "Actually, that's how I first met your dad!"

Brandon was in shock! He couldn't believe what he was hearing! "But the good thing," he said out loud, "is that I am quite good at football, so how hard it could it be?"

Coach Grundle interrupted Brandon. "Oh no! It's not like the easy football you play, young Brandon! No! Intergalactic football involves magic and spells and tricks of magnificent wizardry. You see, the games are played against teams who can invoke spells that can change the speed or direction of the ball, can allow you to breathe under water or jump high and over the opposition like a kangaroo! There is even the black art wizardry which can cause tremendous injuries and is used in the darker realms, although many are trying to have it outlawed. Then, of course, there is the battleground itself! The pitches are divided into sections with revolving challenges. You will have fire-spitting dragons flying overhead, volcanic hot steam geysers that eject lava, water pits that you will need to swim under which have sharks and alligators, and anthills that can devour your boots if you step on them—and I haven't even mentioned the one-eyed charging bulls! No, Brandon, this is like no ordinary game of football. You must train and practice to perfect your skills or you can DIE during the games!"

"DIE?!" screamed Brandon. "Oh my gosh!"

Brandon was trying his best to comprehend all this new information. That's when he remembered Mum and Dad and Safiya at home. He turned to Coach

Grundle and said, "Coach Grundle, my mum will be so worried about me…can we let her know I am ok?"

Coach Grundle explained to Brandon that everything was fine and everyone at home would be kept informed but for now Brandon needed to focus on his training at Doomshot Academy.

CHAPTER 10

New friends

Coach Grundle pointed to the post-registration desk and told Brandon to join the queue of others and collect his papers. He would be told what to do and where to go after that. He assured Brandon he shouldn't worry and told him that he would see him later for assembly. Then Coach Grundle got up and rushed off, disappearing into the crowds.

Brandon walked over to the group that had gathered. He noticed all sorts of different kids of different ages, and some were not even proper humans.

It wasn't long before someone came up to Brandon and started chatting to him. "Hello, my name is Lucy Longtail. What's your name?" Lucy had a look of confidence and determination about her. She was just about as tall as Brandon. She had the most magnificent, thick, luscious red hair that flowed effortlessly. She had what initially looked like a red tattoo along one side of her face that was masked mainly by her hair, but Brandon noticed it went down her neck too.

Lucy smiled and it instantly made Brandon smile in return as he replied, "My name's Brandon."

"First time to the Seventh Realm?" Lucy asked.

"Yep! What about you?" replied Brandon.

"I've been once before with my mum, but I was only three and I don't remember it much, to be honest. Mum talks about it all the time, though, so I knew what to expect. I'm from Valarium District on the Fourth Moon. Where are you from?" Lucy asked Brandon.

"I'm from London…err…from behind the Co-op, I guess?" Brandon replied shyly.

Just as Brandon was about to ask Lucy a question, a tall boy with three eyes came over and interrupted. "Hello!" he said in a warm and gentle voice. "My name is George Dhilian. I'm from the Mayan district." George smiled and both Brandon and Lucy smiled back.

Brandon noticed George's two eyes blinked independently from his middle third eye, and Brandon couldn't help but stare straight into his third eye. It was astonishing. As Brandon looked at George, the allure of his eyes almost hypnotised Brandon. He noticed a starry gaze inside the pupil of his third eye. Brandon suddenly realised he was staring and making George uncomfortable. Brandon introduced himself and Lucy did the same.

The three of them noticed a Minotaur boy standing away from the crowds and looking down at his hooves very shyly and uncomfortably. At this point nothing fazed Brandon. Seeing a minotaur?? *Yeah, ok, that is normal, I guess,* thought Brandon.

The three of them went over and introduced themselves, asking the Minotaur boy what his name was. He raised his head and, with eyes still looking down, quietly introduced himself. "My name is Kronos, Kronos of SubGaia."

Brandon tapped him gently on the shoulder and whispered, "Hey, don't worry, we're all new here too. Why don't you hang out with us!"

Kronos smiled and said, "Thanks!"

Just then they were abruptly interrupted by a screeching siren. Brandon looked up towards one of the two towers flanking the academy building and he saw a flashing red beacon, shooting fire intermittently. Brandon watched as others gathered their belongings and ran into the main doors. He stopped one older-looking boy and asked where everyone was going. The boy turned and at looked at Brandon and as he hurried off, he said, "Head to the main assembly hall. They will be announcing which houses the new members will be joining for training season this year!" Then he rushed off.

Brandon grabbed his things, and he, Lucy, George and Kronos hurried behind the crowds and entered a magnificent hall. Brandon's eyes lit up like fireworks on the fifth of November as he looked around the magnificent hall.

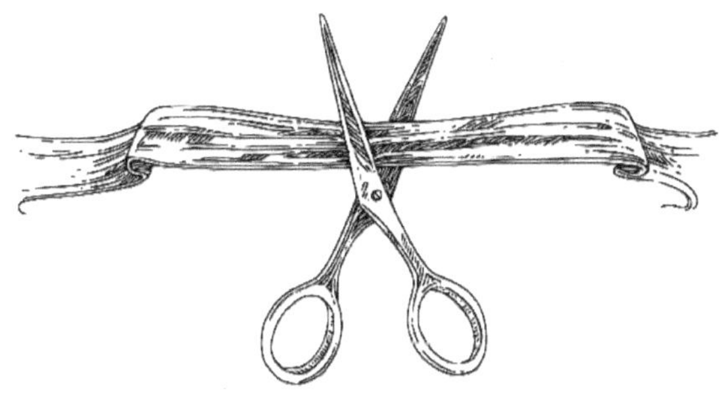

CHAPTER 11

House team ceremony

The inside of the main hall was like an indoor palace designed like a grand national stadium. The main hall had huge ceilings. The walls reached high and curved effortlessly, merging into the ceiling. The ceiling itself looked like the sky but as you looked closely you could see it was artificial and shimmered digitally, as if it was a TV or computer screen or projection. The sides were draped with silky long curtains that had different patterns, like flags, but none that Brandon recognised. The corners of each room had long gold columns upon which gold open bowls were well balanced, and a flame flickered gently but brightly from each. A stage and podium faced the main seating. It was similar to what Brandon was used to seeing in his own school, but this was much grander, with red wood and ivory-coloured trim. In the centre section opposite the main stage were four areas with their own dugouts and benches surrounding them.

As everybody settled down, taking a seat on the benches that lined the big hall, a fearsome-looking man, who looked as if he was made entirely from gold, stood at the front of the hall, shimmering from the reflection of the hall lights. He blew on his whistle to gain everybody's attention. The noise of chit-chatting that had filled the room suddenly turned to silence.

"My name is Coach Jules Remit, and I am the Head Coach of the Intergalactic Football Training at Doomshot Academy," he said in a deep and confident voice. "It is always a pleasure to welcome you all as I look out and see the faces of so many new students and of course to see our former students return.

"Now I want to explain what will happen. This morning, we will perform one of our most important traditions, a ceremony that dates to the ages, and to the origins of Doomshot Academy. All new students will be allocated to train within one of the four prestigious houses' teams." Coach Remit pointed to the four team benches that occupied the four corners of the room. In beautiful calligraphy above each dugout bench were the names Betelgeuse, Rigel, Aldebaran and Sirius.

"The selection ceremony is ordained through a penalty shootout ceremony here in the grand football pitch hall," continued Coach Remit. "When you step up to take your penalty, close your eyes and project your true self, and the process will place you in the right house. It is essential for your training that you are true to yourself, as being placed on the correct house team will best support your training through the seasons."

Brandon watched as one by one, each new student stepped up. As they approached, they would close their eyes and imagine their 'true self', just as Coach Remit had advised. But as they each stepped up to take their turn, as they closed their eyes and then opened them to take the penalty, they were faced with ghastly beasts that appeared as the goalkeeper. As each student stepped up, they focused and found their way to overcome this beastly goalkeeper and score. As the ball whizzed past each ghastly beast and struck the back of the net, the student would be swirled around in a cyclone of colourful winds and would land on the bench of the house they had been selected to join.

Brandon watched as Lucy stepped up, then George, then Kronos and finally it was Brandon's turn. He stepped up, looking relaxed but concentrating. He closed his eyes and then was opposed by a huge beast that looked like a polar bear with fangs. Brandon opened his eyes, looked the beast straight in the eyes and ran towards the ball on the spot. He switched his eye to the bottom right corner and kicked the ball with his left outer foot. The ball curled into the top left corner, completely fooling the Beast. As the ball smashed into the net, Brandon was sucked up in a whirlwind and dropped onto the bench of Rigel. Huge cheers came from the rest of the Rigel House, and Brandon smiled. He looked across and saw his new friends were close by.

As the final new student was placed into their house, Coach Remit explained that they should all retire to their rooms because the next few weeks would be full of intense training in the magical arts of football wizardry. There would be eleven rotations and they would need to pass each of the tests at the end of each rotation. At the end of the intense training sessions, only the exceptional individuals would be selected from each house to play in the intergalactic tournament, a tournament that decided the fate of their galaxy.

Brandon and his new friends left the grand hall and went to their dorms. Each corridor was like a player's tunnel and the emergence from each tunnel, either in cross-corridor junctions or into your destination, reminded Brandon of the light as players emerged out into Wembley.

CHAPTER 12

Getting his new kit

Brandon was deep asleep in his bed after his first night in the dorms at Doomshot Academy. The dorms were honeycomb-like structures, like a beehive, each comb creating a sleeping pod built directly into the wall. The entrance of the pod, which you climbed into in order to sleep, was covered by a digital projection of a football, which you could open or close using a small button to the side. This projection, like that which Brandon had seen covering the roof of

Doomshot Academy, kept the sound and cold out, effectively sealing the pod so each person could sleep comfortably. The strains of *Nessun Dorma,* sung by famous tenor Luciano Pavarotti, could be heard quietly playing in the background as the room remained perfectly still.

The covering of Brandon's pod suddenly opened and he was awakened by a floating football that bounced gently on his forehead. The ball turned into an arrow pointing to an electronic scoreboard mounted on the wall of every room. On the board, he saw a note that read, "Brandon - meet Coach Grundle immediately in his office". Brandon jumped out of bed, got changed and went to meet Coach Grundle by following the floating football that moved along the corridor. It was a dimly-lit corridor with digital photos hanging on the wall. These photos had 3D images with some of the most famous goals from the world cup and from players and planets that Brandon had never seen before, but truly impressive goals!

Brandon soon arrived at a door that had a picture of Coach Grundle holding a trophy on it. Brandon knocked on the door, and the picture of Coach Grundle came to life and in a South American accent a long scream of 'Goooooooooooooooooooooooal!' was heard. The door opened and Coach Grundle was sitting at his desk. He signalled with his hand for Brandon to come in and sit down while he typed away on his laptop. Coach Grundle's office was a mess. He had trophies and medals hanging off every piece of furniture. On all the walls, there were old pictures of Coach Grundle, standing with different people, some accepting a trophy and some team photos. There were piles and piles of books. Handwritten notes with strategy and formation pictures were scattered across the floor. Coach Grundle pushed the pile of books out of the way, pulled a chair close and tapped the seat signalling to Brandon to sit down. Coach Grundle asked Brandon if he slept well and Brandon replied, "Yes sir."

Coach Grundle then told Brandon that his dad had

also been in Rigel house and explained the meaning of Rigel. "You see Brandon, Rigel represents those select few souls whose internal aura shines so brightly they light up the galaxy as a guiding light against the darker forces for the lost ones."

Brandon looked at Coach Grundle strangely but shrugged as if to say, "Yeah, ok, sure."

Coach Grundle asked Brandon if he had his kit yet, but Brandon explained he didn't have anything. He said he wasn't exactly prepared for this! Coach Grundle said not to worry; he would help him arrange everything. Coach Grundle said, "Let's go shopping, Brandon!"

Coach Grundle made round circular movements with his right foot, then tapped the spot three times. He mumbled an incantation and suddenly a wormhole opened, and Brandon could see his home high street. Coach Grundle and Brandon stepped into the wormhole and they both appeared back in London outside a Sport Direct shop.

Brandon looked at Coach Grundle and said, "You must be joking, right?"

Coach Grundle just laughed. They entered Sports Direct and headed to an area behind the golf clubs and camping gear. Coach Grundle showed Brandon a special door through the changing rooms which they entered. They now entered a secret section of Sports Direct and Brandon noticed kits according to his house teams at Doomshot Academy, and lots of other team kits he had never seen before. He saw kits that had three arm sleeves and shorts for Minotaurs and jerseys that had openings for dragons' wings.

Coach Grundle instructed Brandon to get measured up by standing in front of a magic digital mirror. A digital face appeared and greeted Brandon by name. Red and green lasers projected out from the mirror and scanned Brandon's body from head to toe and then, using what looked like a 3D printer, produced a full kit, including shin guards, perfectly made for Brandon.

Brandon was gobsmacked. "That was awesome!" he

shouted in delight. "Mum always buys me kits that are too big! Great to get one that fits just perfect!"

Next, Coach Grundle took Brandon to a side room that had boxes and boxes of boots. Coach Grundle told Brandon to imagine his favourite player and favourite goal of the season. As Brandon closed his eyes and began imagining this, the room lit up and all the shelves began to shake. A box fell from the top shelf and a pair of Adidas Predator boots fell to his feet. As Brandon opened the box, the boots began to glimmer.

Coach Grundle smiled and looked at Brandon. He then told Brandon with real pride in his voice, "These boots have chosen you!"

Coach Grundle then looked at his Fitbit watch and told Brandon they must hurry back to Doomshot Academy - training was about to start. He conjured up another wormhole and both jumped through and returned to Doomshot. Brandon ran off to the sports hall, ready for his first training rotation.

CHAPTER 13

Virtual reality training chambers

Brandon entered the main sports hall and looked around the room for Lucy, George and Kronos. He saw Kronos first, as his body and head towered above all the others. Brandon ran over to the group, smiling with pride as he showed off his new kit and boots to the others. The smiles were reciprocal as each of them showed their kits off too. They were interrupted when a slim but muscular looking lady blew hard and loud on her whistle. She called everyone to attention and began to explain what was going to happen next.

"My name is Coach Slamdunk and I will be your rotation coordinator during your 11 sessions and tests." Coach Slamdunk pointed down each one of the dark corridors, towards what looked like entrances to caves. "You will enter incredibly sophisticated virtual reality, or VR, simulation chambers. Each simulation chamber contains a series of challenges aimed at perfecting your skills and teaching you the art of combining football with the magic arts that will be needed to overcome your opposition."

George raised his hand and asks Coach Slamdunk, "What's a VR simulation chamber??"

Coach Slamdunk explained, "It's a room full of make-believe things. Imagine, for example, if you could step through a TV screen directly into your favourite computer game and join in the game. That's exactly what a simulation chamber is!"

There were lots of "oohs" and "aahs" from the

group of very impressed children.

"Each one of you will have to master all 11 core skills in order to successfully pass your training at Doomshot Academy." Coach Slamdunk explained to the group. "At Doomshot Academy, in order to truly master the arts, one must settle the mind, channel the inner core energy that unites every living being to the One Source Energy and ensure they cast the spells they will soon begin to learn at the exact right moment."

Coach Slamdunk further explained, "As you settle your mind, you will feel all the energy channelling through the body from the crown chakra down towards the right boot." She moved her hand from her head to her boots. "Your boots, you see, have a special power that enables you, their wearer, to channel supreme energy into executing the move to incredible perfection. The spell, an incantation, must be cast at the right time, or things can certainly get interesting…and hilarious!" Coach Slamdunk laughed out loud...but no-one was laughing with her. Instead they stared back in confusion.

Brandon looked across at Kronos and as they exchanged looks, fear changed to excitement. Coach Slamdunk continued, "I must be honest, not all of you will be able to handle what awaits you down these corridors. That's ok. We will be watching and will intervene if it gets too much. At this stage we are looking to build our strongest, smartest, most daring squad."

At that point, Coach Slamdunk blew her whistle and shouted, "Good luck, students!"

Brandon was then directed down the first long and dark corridor by a floating ball. Brandon looked worried as he headed into the darkness.

CHAPTER 14

Spells, bulls and fire-breathing Dragons

As Brandon cleared the darkness from the corridor and got closer to the other side, he saw a light and then entered a dome-shaped chamber. The main pod of the chamber had cushioned seating all around the edge against the white soft-cushioned walls. The whole area looked like the inside of a giant inflatable balloon. The walls were broken up by a metallic door that had a scanning device that opened upon facial recognition. The floor was hard and cold and as each student entered, the echoing sound reverberated around the room.

A robotic voice came from the speakers in the corner of the room. "In this rotation training you will be practicing dribbling... I am the virtual referee and I will be examining your skills. I don't make mistakes, so please don't try and argue with my decisions or you will be removed and will instantly fail this test. Is that understood?"

Brandon, along with all the students, replied with a firm head nod.

The VR asked who wants to go first. Brandon thought to himself, *I'm great at dribbling. I'm happy to go first.*

He put his hand up and the VR announced, "Very well, young Brandon, please enter the simulation chamber doors."

Brandon entered, and the doors closed behind him.

He could no longer see or hear anyone else outside, although the walls turned into one-way windows and all the other kids could still see *him* through the one-way looking glass!

The VR projected three incantations on the wall and asked Brandon to read and memorise them. The VR explained, "The first one will help you to float on water if you see a deep pool or lake, or you need to cross a large area of water. The second one will allow you to go under the water and will let you dribble below the water and keep breathing like a fish. The final one will allow you to triple your pace if you need a sudden boost. This will only give you five-second boosts and please use it carefully, as it will use a lot of your energy. Understood?"

Brandon was now looking less confident than when he first agreed to go inside and was wondering why and when he would need these spells.

The VR announced to Brandon, "In here, you will need to successfully learn to dribble across the pitch, avoiding snapping crocodiles and fire-spitting dragons and fearsome beasts that are common on the higher level DefCon pitches."

Brandon looked up in shock and shrieked, "What??!"

Before he could protest any more, the VR counted down, "Three, two, one..." then the room changed into a fiery pitch with flying creatures and ghastly beasts roaming all around.

A ball appeared at Brandon's feet and he saw in the distance a goal with an arrow pointing him to come over. Brandon began dribbling, thinking this was not so bad. Suddenly, a shooting lightning bolt struck to his right. Brandon flicked the ball over his foot and shimmied it past two slithering snakes and moved away from the danger zone. *This is NOT going to easy, but you can do this,* Brandon said to himself.

Suddenly Brandon came to the edge of a pool and there was nowhere left for him to go. "How will I get across now?" thinks Brandon! Then he remembered the spells. He decided he would use the spell to dribble across the water...but just at that moment, a fire-breathing dragon swooped down and almost bit Brandon's head. Brandon thought quickly and decided it might be better for him to go down under the water and avoid that dragon.

Brandon chanted the spell. "#footballosio – breathingosio – gillsosio – goooooalio#"

He looked down and his boots began to glow. He moved towards the water and walked in until his head was completely covered. *Amazing! I can breathe normally,* thought Brandon.

He continued to dribble through, passing a turquoise glowing octopus and big rocks. He avoided a three-headed shark and kept dribbling forward... then he saw the countdown clock above the surface of the water and realised time was going to be up soon, so Brandon crossed the last area and came back out on to land. Suddenly, when Brandon was literally ready to reach the goal, a giant red one-eyed bull came charging from behind. Brandon remembered the pacing spell, closed his eyes and chanted the spell.

"#speedioso – ronaldosio – muscloscio – goooolio#"

His boots once again lit up and with incredible speed he zoomed past the charging ball and, with a mighty kick, smashed the ball with four seconds remaining on the clock.

Brandon collapsed to the ground, completely out of breath. The doors opened, and the others cheered Brandon for an amazing performance. Brandon smiled as he realised he had completed the test successfully!

The VR announced the next student to enter. Brandon was told to go and rest inside a cryochamber, a small box that he sat inside that covered everything except his head and contained the most incredible black and gold ice cubes, designed to help his muscles relax and recharge.

Later that evening, all the students were chatting about what an amazing and scary experience they had. Coach Remit announced that tomorrow the sessions would be getting harder.

"Harder!" shrieked Brandon. Everyone turned and laughed at Brandon's shriek and Brandon started smiling!

"For now, eat your dinner and get some rest ready for tomorrow," instructed Coach Remit.

CHAPTER 15

Becoming best friends

Over the next few weeks, all the students continued to move through different rotation session simulation chambers, each with incredible challenges and amazing results.

The sessions included dribbling drills, turning drills, crossing drills, heading drills, tackling drills, passing drills, shooting drills, ball control and footwork drills.

The skills drills were also aligned to corresponding magical spell training drills. Dribbling skills would see a student invoke the python or rattlesnake spell, which would allow a player to literally slither through and past an oncoming defender. Heading skills could be combined in perfect combination with a kangaroo spell, allowing a player to jump and leap over and around an obstacle or defender. The students learnt the history of the black arts spells and were warned about never using such spells, even when tempted. Such black art spells included the studsfirst spell or sliding puma spell. Such spells had caused players to become seriously injured and could lead to permanent expulsion from the Academy.

Brandon, Lucy, George and Kronos became great friends during this time. They would meet up regularly for lunch and dinner. All the time they'd be telling each other about their home life, about their experiences in the simulation chambers, and sharing different stories. They were often seen falling over laughing at jokes that Brandon loved to tell everyone.

Kronos described his session in the pacing

simulation. "...and then, just after clearing the four blue cobras and the fire breathing dragons, outpacing the killer kangaroos and thinking I'm totally invincible, a crab bites me on my bottom and I scream in agony!" Kronos burst out laughing and so did everyone else.

George described his embarrassing moment in the crossing simulation. "I was sure I had the crossing nailed. I have a gift for seeing lengths and widths in a strangely easy way. I was running down the wing, looked up, saw the beastly goalkeeper standing away from the line, so I looked up, measured the distance and went to cross the ball. BUT...I wasn't looking where I was running, and two seemingly cute possums pop up out of nowhere; they've tied my laces together and now I'm tripping over, fall head first into what looked like a pot hole, but it was actually the shell of a turtle. When I get up, I'm running with a shell on my head, I can't see anything, and I fall again, but as I fall, my foot kicks the ball, it hits a tree on the left and curls in and goes over the goalkeeper and it scores! Of course I told VR that I meant to do all of that!"

Lucy described how she completely smashed it in the volley simulation. "I don't think anyone had a chance to catch me. When I shimmied past that pack of blood thirsty wolverines and dodged the snapping alligators in the swamp water, I knew I had to flick the football and using keepie-uppies, I got past the razor-sharp grass. I must admit, I was worried about the final volley, so I rolled the ball over my left foot, kicked it up against that giant tree and as the ball came bouncing back to me...*BOOM*...I smashed it on the turn and the ghastly beast goalkeeper had no chance. I'm glad I remembered the tornado kick incantation spell too"

Everyone was just staring at Lucy as she described her experience. Then Brandon said, "I don't think anyone is going to mess with you!" He laughed. There was a strange silence, then Lucy burst out laughing too.

Brandon started thinking about his little sister and told the gang all about her. Brandon thought they would love Safiya. Even though they fought a lot, Brandon misses her so much. Lucy and Kronos put their arms around Brandon and told him to remember that he'll see her soon.

Lucy told the group she's an only child and always wanted to have a brother or sister.

Kronos explained that he had an older brother, but he went to fight in the Rebellion Games and unfortunately never returned. He missed him a lot. The group told Kronos they were sure he'd be so proud of him if he could see him now.

The group carried on sharing jokes and stories until late in the night, when the whistle blew, telling everyone to head to bed. Tomorrow would be the final training session and potentially the most difficult challenge... Penalty Shootouts...

Brandon was excited. He couldn't wait for this one. He headed to bed and fell asleep after such a tiring day.

CHAPTER 16

The fear of penalties

Coach Remit addressed the group. "When you first joined Doomshot Academy, your initiation ceremony and entrance into your respective house teams was determined by taking a penalty. Do you remember the ghastly beast goalkeeper you had to beat? The true meaning of this was to face your inner demons, to understand that the ultimate battle we all face every day is to face the challenges that could hold us back from accomplishing our greatest works.

"Each one of you here today has overcome one challenge or another. Whether it's the anger that rages inside you, the fear of loneliness, the worry of passing your exams or the desire to find the courage to do the right thing when no one is looking...Well...I'm here to tell you that you are going to need to build your confidence, focus your mind and believe in yourself! Penalties in the Seventh Realm and the intergalactic tournaments are manifestations of overcoming your deepest fears and worries."

Coach Remit continued, "When you step up and take that penalty, you are stepping up to take on that which you fear the most. You must settle your mind, pick your spot and as your foot connects with the ball, you will feel time slow down and that which you fear the most will become a reality. You will then have a one-to-one battle with your deepest fear. If your fear defeats you, your penalty will be saved.

"Now I want each of you to enter the simulation

chamber and practice over and over. Pick your spot, focus and channel your energy from the crown chakra to the tip of your boot and connect. I cannot emphasize enough how important and dangerous this skill will be for you all.

"Many of the greatest graduates from Doomshot Academy have gone back to their worlds and suffered great pain and losses because they could not master this core skill."

As Coach Remit concluded his instructions and guidance, the students all went one by one to the simulation chambers. The halls were filled with cries of pain, groans and finally cheers of joy, and by the evening, everyone was exhausted.

Brandon picked up his boots bag and swung it over his shoulder. He had put everything he had into these training sessions and final assessments. There was nothing more that he could have given. Exhausted but pleased with his overall discipline and performances, Brandon began to think about the training drills he had at school for the squad selection back home. He remembered that he had given everything he had even then, but because of lack of discipline which caused him to get into a fight with the other boy, he had lost out on a place in the team. Brandon knew nothing like this happened this time, but he also was aware anything could happen.

Brandon left the chambers and headed straight to bed. Tomorrow was finally a rest day and preparations for the grand pre-selection party were all underway. Brandon was totally excited to find out who would be selected for the squad to play in the intergalactic tournament.

CHAPTER 17

Rumours of trouble from the Darkside

As the final training rotations were completed and everyone anxiously awaited the decision from the Supreme Council of Doomshot Academy for the announcement of the final squad line-up, the grand party preparations were underway. Decorations were being put up and everyone was excitedly getting their outfits ready for the big night of fun.

Lucy and Brandon, all dressed up and looking beautiful, elegant and handsome, walked down the corridor to meet up with George and Kronos. They were talking about the party but also about making the squad.

Brandon told Lucy, "I know we're young and only a few of the young ones get selected so early, but I'm so excited about it. I'm scared too. I've heard rumours about how rough the teams from the darker realms play. I even heard they cheat a lot."

Lucy agreed that she'd also heard the same rumours.

As Brandon and Lucy turned the corner of the corridor, they saw George and Kronos peering into a door of the staff room. Brandon was about to ask what they were doing when George turned and motioned for them to be quiet and just listen. Inside the room, the staff of Doomshot Academy was in a secret meeting. Brandon heard Coach Remit telling everyone, "I've heard from the Leaders of the Supreme Council that forces from the Dark Realm planets are plotting a takeover during the football qualifications Intergalactic Tournament." Coach Remit explained he was not sure of the details but the Supreme Council was now extremely worried and was making plans to defend the Seventh Realm planets and, of course, the One Source Energy. He told the staff they needed to keep the news top secret so as not to scare all the people and cause panic throughout the realms. Coach Remit told the staff in order to keep everyone calm, the intergalactic tournament needed to go ahead as planned and Doomshot Academy needed to ensure success. Their success at that tournament would squash the Forces from Darker Realms' plans.

Just then a mouse ran over Kronos' foot and he screamed. The staff heard and realised someone was listening. Brandon told the gang to hurry back to his room. There they discussed what they just heard.

"We have to help here, guys!" said Brandon. "The Supreme Council will know how to deal with the darker planets and there's nothing we can do for that...but we can certainly make sure we help win the intergalactic tournament and ensure the Seventh Realm planets keep control of the One Source Energy away from the darker realm planets!"

The three of them looked at Brandon and said, "Yes, let's do this! Let's get a plan together and go to meet Coach Grundle."

CHAPTER 18

The grand party

Fresh from making their pact, Brandon, Lucy, George and Kronos all headed down to the main hall, where the grand party was about to start.

The hall was decorated with beautiful drapes that looked like flags of countries, but Brandon didn't recognise them as flags that he knew. Lucy explained, "These are the flags of the confederation of Seventh Realm planets."

Along the sides of the hall, above the benches, are floating footballs in all different colours and spinning without any devices. Past the array of spinning footballs there are ice sculptures, made from black ice, silver ice, pink ice and blue ice. The ice sculptures resembled players in various positions executing some of the 11 core skills the students had been learning.

Fire lanterns, like those seen at the Olympics, lit and warmed the room in each of the corners. A live band played gentle music. The band members were a variety of uniquely talented individuals. The trombonist had three arms and was playing the harp at the same time. There was a tall Minotaur playing the piano and with his back legs he had percussion instruments playing.

Kronos was beginning to skip to the beat and asked Lucy to come and dance with him. They headed off and signalled George and Brandon to join. Brandon was preoccupied with what he heard earlier. Brandon wanted to go and find Coach Grundle and ask his advice. Brandon told the others he'd join them later, but he must do something for now.

George grabbed a large cylinder flask that had smoking green Vimto, a Seventh Realm favourite drink, and politely declined the invitation to dance, explaining that his feet and eyes were very much made for football and not dancing!

Brandon spotted Coach Grundle in the side dugout and ran over. "Hi Coach Grundle!" he said very enthusiastically.

Coach Grundle was distracted and didn't even notice Brandon until Brandon waved his hand in his direction. "Oh, sorry young Brandon, I didn't notice you there," said Coach Grundle. "Having fun?"

Brandon nodded his head. He then asked Coach Grundle about the threats from the darker realm planets. Coach Grundle asked Brandon how he knew about this. Brandon explained that the rumours were everywhere. Coach Grundle took Brandon to one side. "Yes, they're true, but don't spread them because it will just cause panic, ok?"

Brandon asked what he could do to help. "I want to help and so does the group! We know that the Supreme Council will have plans, but on the pitch, we can make a difference!"

Coach Grundle tapped Brandon on the head and thanked him. "Well, let's wait for the squad announcement and we'll formulate a plan, ok?"

"Yes, sure" replied Brandon.

"Now go enjoy the rest of the party," said Coach Grundle to Brandon.

CHAPTER 19

The squad is announced

The next day, Brandon woke up, rubbed his eyes and looked over at his alarm clock. It was 5.55am. Brandon didn't sleep too well and had been tossing and turning all night. He was anxious because today was the day they'd announce who would be selected to play in the intergalactic tournament. Although the finals which would decide who would control the One Source Energy were still four years away, the qualifications were as important if not more, given that only the qualifying teams could directly protect their planet realms.

To make matters more intense, Brandon had heard rumours that only a handful of players from the first year had ever been picked so young and he was anxious about whether he would be selected.

Brandon dressed in his ceremonial kit, as all students had been advised to do for this morning's ceremony.

After breakfast, Brandon headed straight to the main hall and sat in the Rigel dugout bench area. Coach Remit announced that this morning they would be joined and honoured by some very special guests.

He began by announcing, "And from planet Earth we have three legends, Pele, Keegan and Cruyff." All three entered through wormholes that opened from different parts of Earth. Brandon had a look of amazement on his face. Dad had talked about these legends growing up, but Brandon had no idea that they had all played in the intergalactic tournaments.

The ceremony began and all the strongest and most expected players' names were selected. Cheers of joy and clapping filled the room for the next 45 minutes.

As the special guests got down to the last three names to be included, Brandon looked across at his friends. They knew this was it. None of them had been called out yet and the tension was unbearable. Then as Keegan approached, he picked number 11. The ball whizzed up high into the ceiling and smashed into the chart. The board spelt out...Brandon's name!! Brandon fist-punched the air and screamed a mighty "YES!" Next was Lucy's turn! And the final place went to…Kronos!

As he was about to jump for joy, he turned and looked at George. He hadn't been picked! The group gathered around, but George said he was ok and that he was relieved because he was scared about playing in the tournament against the teams from the Darkside. He told them, "Go join the others; this is your moment.

I'll be watching and supporting you all from the side lines, don't worry!"

Brandon, Lucy and Kronos joined the others on the podium for the final bow.

Coach Remit said in a loud and proud voice, "Allow me to introduce the squad for the intergalactic tournament qualifications for Doomshot Academy!"

Everybody started cheering and whooping. Brandon was so proud! The squad were told to go and get measured up for new kits. They had a few days' rest and should use this time to perfect their skills and magical incantations to be ready for the qualification tournament games.

CHAPTER 20

Coach Remit's battle cry

Over the last few days, Brandon had been joining the newly selected squad as they discussed strategies about who they were going to play and their strengths and weaknesses. Brandon also had to attend intense magic lessons and learn incantations from the playbook and think about when and how to use the right spells.

There was a lot to learn and at times the players felt overwhelmed and anxious. Coach Grundle and Coach Slamdunk did an amazing job coaching them on the power of positive thinking and remembering the bigger picture.

The day of the tournament finally arrived. As they all sat in the changing rooms, Coach Remit came in. He gathered everybody and called for their full attention by blowing hard on his whistle. "Ok team," began Coach Remit, "this is it. You've all trained so hard and you deserve this place. But now it's all about what happens in the next few games. You need to dig deep, think of everyone who sacrificed for you to be here, and think of your families back home, relying on you to win to protect their way of life. I cannot tell you anything that you don't already know, but I can tell you that these battles will influence generations to come. The peace of the galaxy depends on ensuring control of the One Source Energy remains in the Seventh Realm planets and is not lost to the darker realm planets who would use it to create chaos."

Coach Remit addressed the experienced players and told them, "You must play with all your skills, with strength, with courage and above all, with dignity. It is a battle and not everyone will respect the code of the intergalactic tournament, but we at Doomshot Academy will!" Coach Remit looked across at the younger recruits. He looked at Brandon, Lucy and Kronos and smiled. "You are all the best of the best. Play like a team, trust your teammates and do what you are best at. That's why you are here, after all!"

The changing room erupted with whoops and clapping. Each team member looked at the others and said, "C'mon, let's do this!"

Brandon followed the squad as they left the changing room and headed up the tunnel out into the gigantic stadium filled with supporters. A huge lion's roar ripped through the air as they emerged.

This was it...the first knockout games were beginning.

CHAPTER 21

Knockout stages and spell binding twists

As each game played and finished, cries of joy and groans could be heard echoing throughout the streets and cities.

Doomshot Academy had to play the Reptilian Rangers first. The game started nervously for both teams. Play was tight and although there were few opportunities, both held possession well. Both teams extended spells and moments of football wizardry that made the fans jump from their seats. In the end it came down to a single moment. A mistake from the right back from the Reptilian Rangers allowed the fearless Doomshot Academy striker, Herculean the Titan, to get in past him and he chipped the ball over the keeper, using an incantation that caused the ball to snake up and around the keeper and slither past the line. The game ended 1-0 to Doomshot Academy.

On the other side of the valley, the Darkside Realm teams were brushing their oppositions aside with aggressive and frightening ease. The scariest of the Darkside Realm teams was known as Aryan Army, a team of huge muscular druids that had deep blue piercing eyes and milky white skin. The players had an intimidating presence and when they grimaced at opponents, their black fangs, draping black hair and blue blood flowing through their pulsating veins created a menacing sight. They used black wizardry spells, some of which were largely no longer taught in other realms because they were dangerous and could cause serious damage. One tactic the Aryan Army used was a piercing screeching sound that would distract the opposing team as they floated the ball past the defence.

Over the next few days, teams began to get knocked out and the qualifying teams progressed through to the next stages.

Brandon, Lucy and Kronos got to warm up during each game and in two games, Brandon came on as a substitute, but just for the last ten minutes and was instructed to slow the play down. In the last game, against the Serengeti Zardlos, Brandon came on and invoked the pacing spell and raced past several Rhinosapiens (half man, half rhino), flicking the ball over his left foot and smashing a volley into the top corner, taking the winning goal just before the whistle blew.

As each game passed and teams were knocked out, Doomshot Academy became stronger and more disciplined. They had reached the final game, and it came as no surprise when the last team to reach was announced as Aryan Army. The final battle would be Doomshot Academy vs. Aryan Army.

Meanwhile, whilst the games had been playing, a dark storm had been gathering in the skies. The Supreme Council of Doomshot Academy had been meeting every night, and Brandon, Lucy, Kronos and George would also meet up late at night and sneak out to listen to the meetings.

CHAPTER 22

The Darkside threats grow more worrying

The night before the final game between Doomshot Academy and Aryan Army, a most important and secret meeting was being held in the staff training room of Doomshot Academy. All the staff had been summoned and members of the Supreme Council had also been called to attend. Brandon, Lucy, George and Kronos had snuck out of bed and were crouching in the corner of the top window, where they could see and hear everything that was being said.

As Brandon peered through the small window, he could see the staff gathered round in a huddle. The darkened room was lit only by a few handheld candles. This created shadows that stooped across the floor and up the far wall. Coach Remit led the discussion. "We've now heard that the Potus Emperor of the Dark Realms has been using the distraction of the intergalactic tournaments to gather and build an evil and beastly army to storm the One Source Energy Temple. He intends to take control. He intends to bring this army in to the Seventh Realm when and if the Aryan Army wins the final game."

"As you all know," Coach Remit continued, "the winning team is provided open border permission for all fans to attend the winning ceremony. It would be against intergalactic laws to prevent entry. If they win, the full secret army from the Dark Realms, pretending to be fans, will enter our planet and we will be overtaken. Many people will be hurt and even killed.

More importantly, the Potus Emperor would then have full control of the One Source Energy and who knows what will happen once he has control."

The staff all had looks of concern and fear on their faces. Coach Grundle interrupted, "Some of you here were present during the Rebellion Games. I personally played against the Potus Emperor before he sustained the devastating injury to his left metatarsal. As you know, the Emperor was one of the best and most promising wingers in the Seventh Realm. But after the injury, he just couldn't accept that he would not play again. His mindset became very negative. He struggled to adapt to a role in coaching and even after moving to different jobs, he remained angry all the time. When he signed for Aryan Army as their head coach, he turned to the black wizardry skills and many new students were corrupted. I wonder sometimes if there is any of the original Good Emperor left in him; as his eyes have turned deep blue and grey, it is difficult to remember the original brilliant wizard that he was."

Coach Slamdunk joined in the discussion. "Look, there is no time for sentimental stories. The fact is, a real threat exists, and we must prepare ourselves. I have spoken to most of the other Academies and we are pulling together a football squadron alliance to prepare for battle. The bottom line is that we have depleted reserves in the combined arsenal: some exploding football cannons and various other weapons. We also have limited numbers of trained people and it will be almost impossible to gather a strong defence without alarming the people." Coach Slamdunk spoke very quietly but directly at this point. "Ultimately, we need to ensure we win the final. I know we cannot put more pressure on the team beyond what we already have, but if we can win the game, we will foil the Potus Emperor's plans of bringing in his secret army."

Brandon looked at the group and gave them a sign to head back to his room. Once back in the room, Brandon made sure no one was around to overhear the discussion. "We have to use all our training skills and magic spell drills exactly how we have practiced over the last few weeks. We can pull this off and make sure we win the game and thereby ensure we protect the One Source Energy, without anyone getting hurt and without panic spreading throughout the realms."

Brandon looked around, making eye contact with each friend. They all gave each other a look of acknowledgement and shouted out loud, "Let's do it!"

Brandon felt fear and excitement at the same time. "We need to rest now, as tomorrow the fate of the Universe will be decided by our feet."

CHAPTER 23

The final (first half...)

As the sun rose over the awesome fortress building of Doomshot Academy, the streets were beginning to wake up to noise and excitement about the final between Doomshot Academy and Aryan Army. For most people, this was an exciting final game and they were simply thinking about their favourite team winning the trophy.

But as Brandon woke up, he had a troubled look on his face. He and the gang were aware of the fate of the Seventh Realm planets, the fate of the One Source Energy temple and the fate of the lives of so many people, which all depended upon them winning the game today…

Brandon jumped out of bed, got into his training tracksuit and headed off, deep in thought, and despite the noise and excitement, he remained distant in his own thoughts.

The players had already started going over the playbook and Coach Remit had given his important motivational prep talk. As the players, all whooping, exited the changing rooms, they headed up the players' tunnel toward the pitch.

As Brandon, Lucy, Kronos and the rest of the players emerged from the tunnel there was a loud eruption of cheers from the crowd. They walked out and acknowledged the applause of their fans and then focused on their warm-up routine, which they had practiced a thousand times before.

The star striker for Doomshot Academy, Herculean the Titan, was pacing and stretching up and down the sidelines when someone passed the ball to him, and as he stepped out to control the ball, he slipped on a large object that was sticking out of a small pothole. It was a fallen extracted SabreGator (half tiger, half alligator) tooth which had not been cleared from a previous game. Herculean fell to the ground in agony. The physio and doctor rushed over and were seen telling Coach Grundle that he was badly injured and would not be able to continue. Everyone was shocked and devastated. Herculean had scored the most goals for Doomshot Academy so far and they were relying on him for this game!

Coach Grundle rushed over to Brandon and pulled him to one side. "Ok Brandon, this is not exactly what we all discussed in the game book, but you have that special touch, and although you are still young, I believe in YOU. I want you to start the game and take Herculean's place."

Brandon looked nervously at Coach Grundle. "Are you sure this is a good idea?? I know what is at stake here, Coach!"

Coach Grundle assured Brandon this was most definitely the right move and that he had full confidence in him. He then looked Brandon in the eye and asked him, "The question is, do you have confidence in yourself? Believe what you know is your destiny, Brandon, and unlock the doors to your SUPER-SELF!"

Brandon formed a fist with his right hand, shook it confidently, and replied, "Yes sir, I won't let you down!"

Brandon got into his kit and, wearing his proud number 11 shirt, he began warming up. He scanned the crowd of hundreds of thousands in attendance, and he started to think about Dad and how he always came to watch his games back in London. He wished at that moment that Dad could be there. Dad always knew how to give him the confidence to go for it and seeing his face gave Brandon the courage he sometimes needed. He also wished Mum and Safiya were there too, with Mum holding a snack—a drink that only she knew how to make perfectly for him. This time, no one was around, and Brandon would just have to get on with it without them. He focused his mind and started on his drills.

Suddenly the skies above turned grey and dark and there was another roar from the crowds. The Aryan Army players emerged from the tunnel and entered the pitch. As they walked past the Doomshot squad and coaches, they growled and snarled and flexed their muscles to intimidate the Doomshot players. They moved slowly and began a practiced routine of chanting slogans of war and destruction in their own language.

Coach Grundle told his team to come close and ignore the intimidation of the Aryan Army players. Coach Grundle looked to the sidelines and made eye contact with Coach Remit and the other staff. They all looked nervous and Brandon and Lucy noticed this. Coach Grundle looked back at the starting team and said, "Ok team, this is it. Give it everything you have and don't leave this game feeling that you didn't give it your best. That's all anyone can ask of you. Go get it!"

The team ran out and took their positions. The pitch changed formation and colours several times and pools of bubbling steam pits emerged.

The referee blew the whistle and the game was now underway...

The ball was being passed around nervously between the players. There were very few open plays and the teams held the ball well between them. Suddenly the Aryan right winger invoked a lightning spell and struck at the edge of the Doomshot midfield. As the defender was taken by surprise at the quick move, he panicked and fell backwards, allowing the Aryan winger to collect the loose ball. He flicked the ball and floated it around the defender, passing a hissing steam pit, and elegantly switched it across the field. It was a pinpoint pass to the Aryan centre forward.

The striker snarled at the goalkeeper and red liquid

could be seen dripping from his fangs. As the striker stared menacingly at the keeper, he invoked a hurricane spell, and with a thunderous volley he smashed the ball, which twisted and turned, heading directly into the top corner of the goal. The Aryan Army fans were on their feet and growling at the Doomshot fans as they watched. The goalkeeper invoked an octopus reflex spell, allowing the Doomshot goalkeeper to get just the slightest of tips to the ball and…he saved it!

The game continued and each move created knife-edge tension throughout the stadium.

Now there were just 90 seconds left on the clock and a clever move from the Aryan winger slipped past his marker, curled the ball in and, using a cycle kick spell, scored! 1-0 to Aryan Army…Doomshot players and staff were devastated as the whistle blew for halftime…

The Aryan Army snarled as they marched past the Doomshot players, intimidating them more and more. Both teams left the field and headed for the changing rooms…

CHAPTER 24

The final (second half...)

Led by their fearless captain Imhotep, Doomshot Academy players emerged from the changing room. Each player had a look of concentration on their faces and they looked directly forward, not making eye contact with anyone. There was a feeling of determination in the air, but equally the smell of fear could be sensed.

A huge roar and growling sound was heard as the Aryan players emerged from their changing room.

They snarled and chanted intimidating sounds, trying to make eye contact with the Doomshot players. One Aryan defender squared up to Brandon and said, "I eat little boys like you for breakfast ...Grrrrr..."

Brandon smiled without even looking at him and kept his focus on the tunnel.

Both teams emerged from the players' tunnel out onto the pitch. The crowd went wild. Coach Slamdunk instructed the team to remember the plan and to stick to the playbook. "It's only 1-0 and we have everything to play for."

Then Coach Grundle signalled to Brandon to look over towards the Royal Box, where all the VIP guests were seated. As Brandon scanned the crowd and squinted past the three suns, he saw a familiar face. It was DAD!! Dad winked and gave Brandon a thumbs-up. Brandon was filled with new positive energy and started getting pumped. He didn't know how or even why Dad had managed to get into the Seventh Realms and why he was seated in the royal box, but right now

Brandon didn't care; he was just super happy that Dad was watching him play!

Coach Slamdunk had decided to bring Lucy on for the second half, and she'd taken position on the right wing. The referee instructed everyone to take their position and blew the whistle. For the second half, Doomshot kicked off. The ball was played backwards and already the nerves were kicking in. It was a short ball back to the centre back and the Aryan striker almost intercepted, but fortunately the keeper was aware of the mistake and rushed out to clear the ball, invoking a zebra kick spell which sent the ball zigzagging upfield away from danger. Coach Grundle shouted instructions from the sidelines, basically telling his team to concentrate!

As each side battled hard and avoided the evolving danger zones of steam pits and fire pools, and occasional lightning bolts, the game saw only a few real chances created by both sides, but no one had yet scored again. It was a very close match and it was impossible to predict what was going to happen.

Then, a silly mistake by the Doomshot defender Lancelot let the Aryan striker skip in and collect a loose ball. The striker invoked a "studsfirst spell," an extremely dangerous spell that could seriously injure someone if it connected. Fortunately, the spell missed the player in front of him but allowed the Aryan striker through with an open view of the goal. He snarled as he lifted the ball up with a shimmy and, with the outside of his right foot, smashed the ball. As it curled in the air, it went over the tip of the keeper's fingers and looked like it was going in…but it hit the cross bar and rebounded back into play. There was huge sigh of relief from the crowds and from the Doomshot players too. That was just too close and could have finished them off for good!

Brandon ran over to Lucy and whispered in her ear, "Let's try the Stanley Move!"

The ball was played out from the defender to Lucy on the right wing. Here Lucy invoked the incantation for dragon ball cross spell, measuring up by squinting her left eye. She fired the ball high and looping over the Aryan defence.

Brandon invoked the kangaroo spell and bounced high above everyone. The Aryan defender tried to pull his leg but it was too late; Brandon had cleared him already. Brandon connected with the ball and headed it down with extreme power and precision.

The ball fell perfectly to the feet of the Doomshot striker, who side-foots easily into the back of the net and they scored…it was a goal! That made the score 1-1. The stadium erupted with noise and the Doomshot bench were jumping and screaming to the players. The referee blew his whistle and the ball was back on the centre spot. This game was now very much alive!!

Aryan Army looked shell-shocked. They were simply stunned and began to lose confidence. They were flying in with wild and aggressive tackles. Coach Grundle shouted instructions to the team, explaining that Aryan Army had lost concentration and Doomshot should use this to their advantage.

From a Doomshot throwing, Brandon collected the ball. He saw a fire-breathing anthill and knocked the ball past this to avoid the oncoming Aryan defenders, shimming the ball to elegantly skip past three charging players. Using his pacing skill spell and dance hotstep spell, he was now one-on-one with the goalkeeper. He needed to keep his cool. Brandon heard Dad's voice in his head. He had a flashback and remembered the late night practicing in the garden back at home with Dad. "Control the game by controlling your emotion."

Brandon slowed his breathing and time seemed to slow down. He measured the distance using a sacred geometry trick George had taught him. He spun the ball, lifted it with his left foot and hit it on the half volley. The crowd went completely quiet. Everyone had their eyes on the ball. The ball whizzed and hissed as it spun on its axis and headed towards the goal.

The Aryan keeper was off his line and stumbled to get back, but the ball curled past him and was spinning to the bottom corner. Would it go in? It was too tight to call it. Everyone had their hands over their mouths as they watched with anticipation. The ball hit the bottom right-hand post, dropped back onto the line, and dribbled just over the line before the keeper could get his hand to it.... It was a goooooooooooooooooooooooal!!

Brandon had done it; he'd scored and Doomshot had taken the lead! Everyone was going crazy and jumping up and down. Coach Grundle and Coach Slamdunk were signalling the players to remain calm and get in position. There were only a few seconds left on the clock, but anything could happen.

Aryan Army were being scolded and shouted at by the head coach. They were a mess and no longer looked as organised as they did when they started. They were barely able to kick off from the centre spot when the referee blew the final whistle.

That was it – Doomshot had won the game! Brandon's last-minute goal had won the game, and everyone ran to him and lifted him high up into the air. Brandon, Lucy and Kronos knew this win had just saved the universe.

It was time for the trophy ceremony,

CHAPTER 25

Trophy ceremony and some special guests arrive

Some of the Aryan Army were receiving instructions from the bench side. The coach was fighting and arguing with the officials that decisions were not made correctly and that the game should be replayed. This was, of course, nonsense and bad sportsmanship. The official VR had ruled that the results stood and Doomshot were the winners!

Brandon was now sitting collapsed on the pitch,

feeling exhausted, overwhelmed, and totally overjoyed. *We did it, we did it,* he kept telling himself. He looked over at George in the dugout, sitting with Kronos. They shot a smile and a wink over to him; Brandon responded in kind. Then he saw Lucy. They smiled at each other. Brandon tapped his heart with his left hand and signalled to Lucy. She smiled back and winked too.

Balloons were floating everywhere; streamers were falling from skies as if it was raining ribbons and bright colours...it was a beautiful scene.

Brandon looked around and saw his team all celebrating on the pitch with each other. Half the squad had picked up Coach Grundle and the other half had Coach Slamdunk. They were flipping them up in the air and cheering. "Three cheers for Coach Grundle and Coach Slamdunk! Hip-hip hooray! Hip-hip hooray! Hip-hip hooray!" Coach Remit had come down to the pitch side and was high-fiving and hugging everyone in his sight.

The squad were called to go up and greet the Supreme Council members and receive their winning medals. Brandon saw Herculean the Titan limping and offered him a shoulder to lean on as they went up the steps. The full squad was on the podium and the trophy was lifted to a rapturous roar!

The crowd went wild and cheers of joy and happiness spread around the whole stadium. As Coach Remit stood with the squad, he told them all, "This victory will be remembered in the history books and is of far greater importance than many of you realise!" He looked over to Brandon, Kronos and Lucy and winked.

The team were posing for photos and enjoying the celebration when a wormhole opened in the sky above them. Smoke and bright colours illuminated the edges of the wormhole and as the smoke cleared, a group of individuals began to appear. An announcement was made on the PA system that explained some very special guests were going to be joining the winning team.

Everyone looked to see who had arrived. Brandon looked past the crowds and he saw... Ronaldo, Messi and Salah! Brandon gasped! No way! No way! No way! Brandon was just shocked. These were his football heroes! How were they here?!

The three of them asked people, "Where's Brandon?"

Two players pointed over to Brandon and Ronaldo, Messi and Salah walked over to him. They introduced themselves and Brandon replied, "I know who you are!" They asked Brandon if they could take a photo with the hero of the game and Brandon replied rather too enthusiastically, "Oh my God, yes, pleeeeease!!"

They all laughed and picked Brandon up and put him on their shoulders and took a few photos and selfies together. Ronaldo pulled one picture out of the Polaroid that someone was using and gave it to Brandon. Brandon said that he'd treasure this moment forever and put the photo in his back pocket.

Then Brandon saw Dad. They smiled at each other

and ran over to each other. Dad picked Brandon up and hugged him. "I'm so proud of you, Brandon. You really stepped up today. All the family are looking down today and will be so proud. Granddad is also so proud of you. He heard the results just now."

Brandon looked at Dad and asked him, "How come you didn't tell me about any of this? I've got so many questions! How, what, when, who???"

Dad laughed and said, "Don't worry, Brandon! There's plenty of time for that. Right now, I need to go to work!"

Brandon looked at him. "Are you serious??"

Dad explained that he worked for the intergalactic council security division. The results of today's game had created ripples in the darker realms, and he must go and investigate. Brandon looked amazed "Wow!! Ok, sure Dad, now I understand!! Go! We'll talk later."

After everything settled down and the stadium had emptied out, Brandon remained in the stadium. He took one last look to remember this magical day. He looked intently at the goal post that he scored the winning goal in and then, just as he was leaving, he saw a janitor clearing up. He walked past and said, "Thank you for doing that."

The janitor, who was looking down with a hood covering his face, nodded as if to acknowledge Brandon saying thank you. Brandon then left the stadium and headed back to Doomshot Academy.

The janitor in the tunnel looked up to see if anyone was around. Seeing the coast was clear, he dropped his hood, which had been covering his face. It was a member of the Aryan Army! In his hand, he had a note which he read to himself. "In the event we fail to beat Doomshot Academy in the final today, you must activate plan B... Signed, Potus Emperor."

He then scrunched it up and dropped it near to the bin. The note fell to the floor and blew away in the wind.

The End

www.ingramcontent.com/pod-product-compliance
Lightning Source LLC
LaVergne TN
LVHW091101150826
845673LV00002B/670

* 9 7 9 8 4 0 3 5 0 1 9 8 9 *